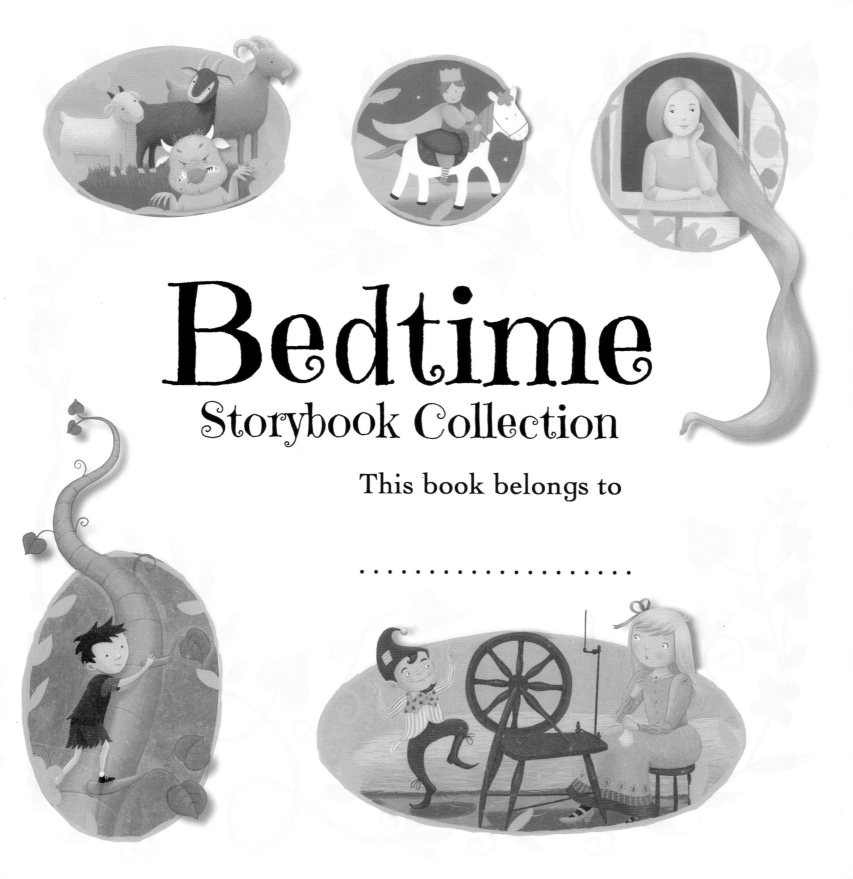

Bedtime
Storybook Collection

This book belongs to

. . . .

This edition published by Parragon Books Ltd in 2015 and distributed by

Parragon Inc.
440 Park Avenue South, 13th Floor
New York, NY 10016
www.parragon.com

ISBN 978-1-4723-9839-0

Printed in China

Bedtime
Storybook Collection

PaRRagon

Bath · New York · Cologne · Melbourne · Delhi
Hong Kong · Shenzhen · Singapore · Amsterdam

Contents

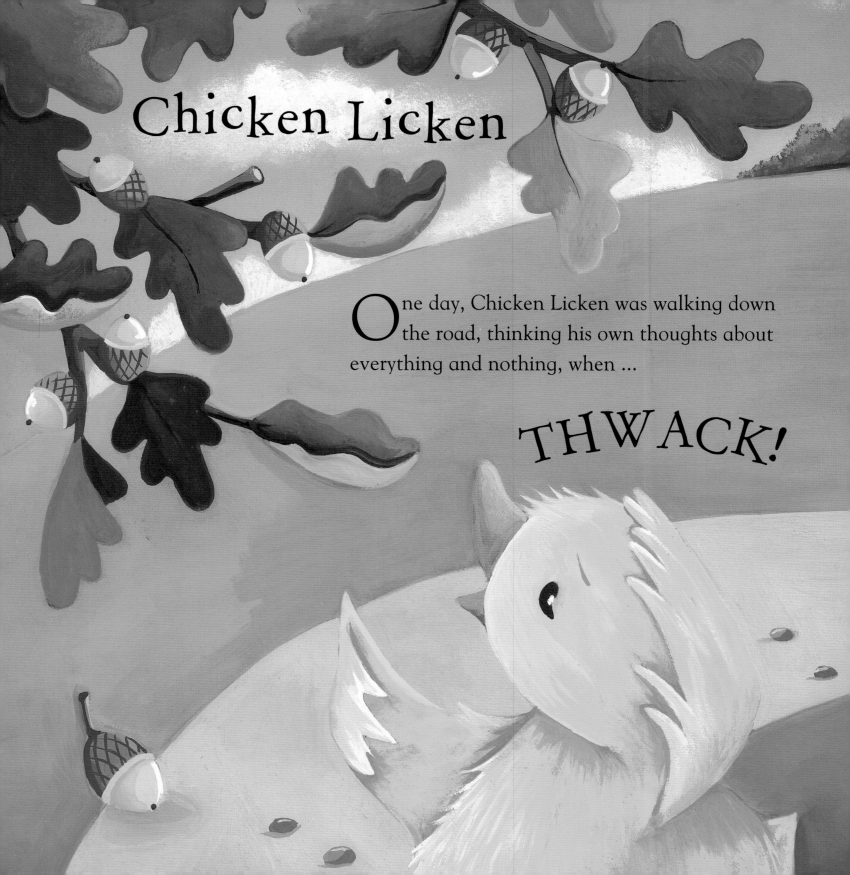

Chicken Licken

One day, Chicken Licken was walking down the road, thinking his own thoughts about everything and nothing, when ...

THWACK!

An acorn fell on his head!

"Ouch!" said Chicken Licken, rubbing his head.
"I think the sky is falling! I must run and tell the king!"

So Chicken Licken ran down the road to tell the king. And on his way he met Henny Penny.

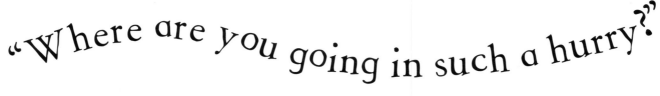

"Where are you going in such a hurry?"

Henny Penny asked Chicken Licken.

"The sky is falling, and I am going to tell the king!" said Chicken Licken.

"I will come with you," said Henny Penny.

So Henny Penny and Chicken Licken rushed down the road to tell the king. And on their way they met Cocky Locky.

"Where are you going in such a hurry?"

Cocky Locky asked them.

"The sky is falling, and we are going to tell the king!" said Chicken Licken.

"I will come with you," said Cocky Locky.

11

So Cocky Locky, Henny Penny, and Chicken Licken dashed down the road to tell the king. And on their way they met Ducky Lucky.

12

"Where are you going in such a hurry?"
Ducky Lucky asked them.

"The sky is falling, and we are going to tell the king," said Chicken Licken.

"I will come with you," said Ducky Lucky.

So Ducky Lucky,

Cocky Locky,

Henny Penny,

and Chicken Licken

scurried down the road to tell the king. And on their way they met Drakey Lakey.

14

"Where are you going in such a hurry?"

Drakey Lakey asked.

"The sky is falling, and we are going to tell the king," said Chicken Licken.

"I will come with you," said Drakey Lakey.

So Drakey Lakey, Ducky Lucky, Cocky Locky, Henny Penny, and Chicken Licken scampered down the road to tell the king. And on their way they met Goosey Loosey.

16

"Where are you going in such a hurry?" asked Goosey Loosey.

"The sky is falling, and we are going to tell the king," said Chicken Licken.

"I will come with you," said Goosey Loosey.

17

So Goosey Loosey, Drakey Lakey, Ducky Lucky, Cocky Locky, Henny Penny, and Chicken Licken hurried down the road to tell the king. And on their way they met Turkey Lurkey.

"Where are you going in such a hurry?"

asked Turkey Lurkey.

"The sky is falling, and we are going to tell the king," said Chicken Licken.

"I will come with you," said Turkey Lurkey.

So Turkey Lurkey, Goosey Loosey, Drakey Lakey, Ducky Lucky, Cocky Locky, Henny Penny, and Chicken Licken raced down the road to tell the king. And on their way they met Foxy Loxy.

"Why, good day, my friends!"

said Foxy Loxy. "And where might you all be going on this fine morning?"

"The sky is falling," said Chicken Licken. "We are going to tell the king!"

21

"Really?

How interesting. Have you ever been to the king's palace before?" asked Foxy Loxy.

"No," said Chicken Licken. The others all shook their heads.

"Then how do you know you will find the way?" asked Foxy Loxy.

"Um … I never thought of that," said Chicken Licken.

23

"Why don't you let me help you?" said Foxy Loxy.

"I know the way to the king's palace very well. Just follow me, and you will be there in no time!"

So Chicken Licken, Henny Penny, Cocky Locky,
Ducky Lucky, Drakey Lakey, Goosey Loosey, and
Turkey Lurkey all followed Foxy Loxy down the road.

25

Soon they came to a path that led into the woods.

They followed Foxy Loxy down the path …

into the woods …

And they never did get to tell
the king that the sky was falling.

The End

The Princess and the Pea

Once upon a time, there was a lonely prince. He lived in a big castle with beautiful rooms and a pretty garden.

30

But he wasn't happy because he didn't have someone special to share them with.

"If only I could find a lovely princess to marry," sighed the prince.

The king and queen did their best to help.
They held balls so the prince
could meet princesses from
all the nearby kingdoms.

The prince danced with tall
princesses and small princesses.

He talked to
LOUD princesses
and proud
princesses.

32

He met all kinds of princesses ...

but none of them was quite right.

After a while, the king and queen ran out of princesses for their son to meet.

"Maybe it's time you went looking for a bride," suggested the queen.

So the prince packed a bag, saddled his horse, and waved goodbye to the king and queen.

"Good luck!" said the king.
"Come back soon!"

The prince traveled far and
wide, and searched high and low
for the princess of his dreams.

35

Along the way, he met lots of pretty princesses.

Princess Grace loved
to dance, but her twirling
made the prince dizzy.

Princess Ginger loved to
cook, but her cakes made
the prince chubby.

Princess Flora loved to smell as pretty as a flower,
but her perfume made the prince sneezy.

ATCHOOOO!

Maybe I'm just too fussy, thought the prince. But in his heart, he knew he hadn't met the princess of his dreams. So he headed back to the castle.

When he got home, the king and queen greeted the prince happily.

"I haven't found a princess yet," he sniffed sadly. "I guess I never will."

"Don't be silly," said the queen, "the right girl will come along soon."

39

That night, there was a terrible storm.
Thunder boomed so loudly that it
rattled the castle's windows.

RATTLE, TATTLE!

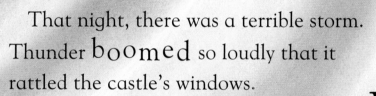

Lightning shook the table as the prince and his
parents sat down to eat their dinner.

40

The prince was just about to help himself to dinner when, suddenly, they all heard a loud ...

RAT-A-TAT-TAT!

Someone was knocking on the door!

"Who could be visiting us on a night like this?" asked the queen.

The prince opened the door and found a very wet girl standing there. Raindrops ran down her muddy cloak, making a puddle at her feet.

Drip!

Drop!

Drop!

Drip!

Drip!

Drop!

Drop!

The girl pushed back her hood and wild curls tumbled out.

"Hello," she said with a smile. "I got lost on my way home and wondered if I could stay here for the night. My name is Princess Polly."

She didn't look much like a princess. But princes must always be polite, so he invited her inside.

Soon the princess was warm and dry.

All night long, rain fell plippety plop, plippety plop on the castle roof. But the prince hardly noticed, because he was too busy talking to Princess Polly.

She was pretty and funny and kind. Princess Polly was everything the prince had hoped to find in a princess.

By the end of the evening,
the prince had fallen in love!

46

But the queen wanted to be sure that the girl really was a princess.

The queen told the servants to pile a bed high with mattresses. They heaved one on top of another until they had no more mattresses left. Then they placed a pillow and blanket right at the top.

Underneath the mattress at the very bottom, the queen placed a teeny, tiny pea.

Only a real princess would be able to feel something so small through all those mattresses!

When the queen showed Princess Polly to her bedroom, the girl gazed up at the tower of mattresses but didn't say anything. She was just grateful to have a bed for the evening.

"Goodnight," said Princess Polly.

"Sleep tight," whispered the queen.

Then Princess Polly changed into her nightgown and climbed right to the top of the pile of mattresses, and snuggled under the blanket.

The next morning, Princess Polly came down to breakfast with dark circles under her eyes.

She let out a great big YAWN!

"How did you sleep, my dear?" asked the queen.

Princess Polly burst into tears.

"I'm afraid I couldn't sleep a wink. There was something **lumpy** and **bumpy** in my bed. It kept me awake all night long!"

To Princess Polly's surprise, the queen clapped her hands with delight.

"So she is a **real** princess!" the queen cried.

The prince was overjoyed.

"Will you marry me, Princess Polly?"

he asked.

"Yes!" squealed the princess.

And they all lived happily ever after!

The End

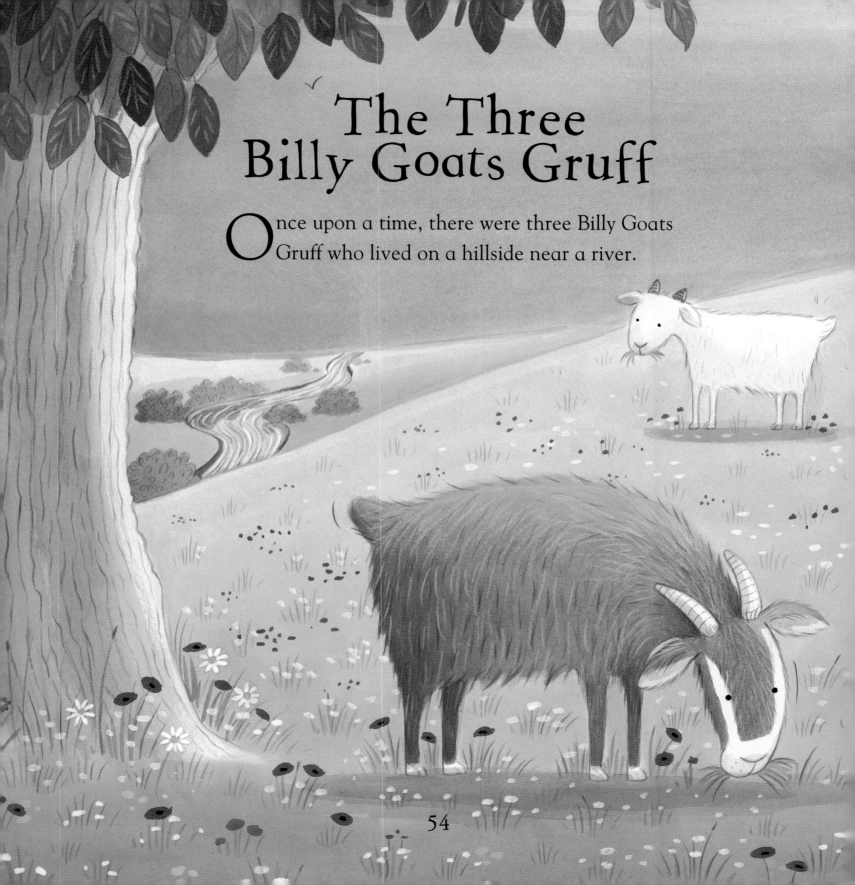

The Three
Billy Goats Gruff

Once upon a time, there were three Billy Goats
Gruff who lived on a hillside near a river.

There was Little Billy Goat Gruff, Middle Billy Goat Gruff, and Great Big Billy Goat Gruff.

They ate the grass on the hillside, and grew fatter and fatter.

One day, the three Billy Goats Gruff looked around and saw that they had eaten all the grass on the hillside!

"What shall we do now?" Little Billy Goat Gruff asked his brothers. "If we don't find more grass, we will waste away!"

"There is plenty of **yummy green grass** over there," said Middle Billy Goat Gruff, looking at a meadow on the other side of the river.

"Yes," said his big brother, Great Big
Billy Goat Gruff. "All we have to do is
cross the wooden bridge, and we can
eat to our hearts' content!"

57

But the bridge was guarded by a horrible, ugly troll.

He was **green** with a **great big head** and a **bright red nose.**

There were **warts on his skin** and **hairs on his chin** and his terrible teeth were **long and pointy and yellow.**

And he was very SMELLY!

58

"Which one of us will be brave enough to cross that bridge?"
Great Big Billy Goat Gruff asked his brothers.

The three Billy Goats Gruff all looked at each other.

At last, Little Billy Goat Gruff piped up, "I will cross the bridge!"

And off he went, down the hillside.

Trip, trap, trip, trap,

he went over the wooden bridge.

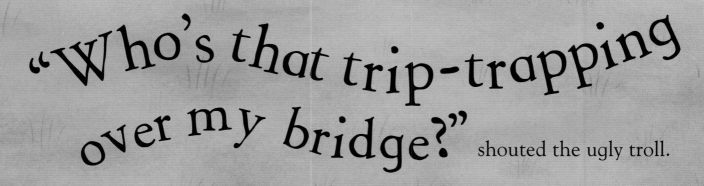

"Who's that trip-trapping over my bridge?" shouted the ugly troll.

"It is I, Little Billy Goat Gruff," the goat replied, trying not to breathe in the troll's horrible smell. "I'm just going over to the meadow to eat the green grass."

"No, you're not!" growled the troll.
"I'm going to eat YOU first!" And he
climbed up on to the little wooden bridge.

63

Little Billy Goat Gruff was very frightened, but he knew what to say.

"I don't think I would make a very good meal for you. Can't you see how little I am? You should wait for my brother, Middle Billy Goat Gruff. He is much **bigger** and **fatter** than me!"

The troll thought about it. **"All right,"** he said. **"You may cross the bridge."**

So Little Billy Goat Gruff went **trip, trap, trip, trap** across the wooden bridge and skipped into the meadow.

65

As soon as he saw that Little Billy Goat Gruff was safe, Great Big Billy Goat Gruff said to his younger brother, "It's your turn now."

So Middle Billy Goat Gruff trotted down the hillside.

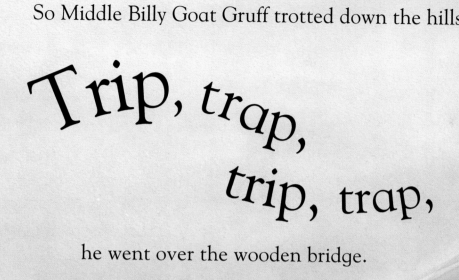

Trip, trap,
trip, trap,

he went over the wooden bridge.

When he was halfway across, the smelly troll shouted,

"Who's that trip-trapping over my bridge?"

"It is I, Middle Billy Goat Gruff," said the goat. "I am just going over the bridge to eat the green grass with my brother on the other side."

"Oh no, you're not," shouted the troll. "I'm going to eat YOU first!" And he climbed right up on to the little wooden bridge.

Middle Billy Goat Gruff was very frightened, but he didn't let the troll see that.

"There's not much meat on my bones," he said. "You should wait for my brother, Great Big Billy Goat Gruff. He is the biggest and fattest of us all, and he would make a much tastier meal for you."

"All right," said the troll. "You may cross the bridge."

So Middle Billy Goat Gruff went

trip, trap, trip, trap

over the wooden bridge to join
his brother in the meadow on
the other side.

At last, it was Great Big Billy Goat Gruff's turn to cross the bridge.

Trip, trap, trip, trap

went his hooves on the wooden bridge.

"Who's that trip-trapping over my bridge?" bellowed the troll.

72

"It is I, Great Big Billy Goat Gruff.
I am going to join my brothers to eat
the green grass in the meadow."

"Oh no, you're not!"
thundered the troll.

"You are the biggest,
fattest Billy Goat
Gruff, and I'm going
to eat YOU!"

And the smelly troll clambered up
onto the bridge.

Great Big Billy Goat Gruff was not afraid of the horrible, ugly troll. But the troll was certainly afraid when he saw Great Big Billy Goat Gruff! He tried to run away, but before he could, Great Big Billy Goat Gruff lowered his head, stamped his hooves and, with his great big billy goat horns, he butted the troll right into the river!

The troll went under the water with a great big

SPLASH

and was never, ever seen again.

Then Great Big Billy Goat Gruff went

trip, trap, trip, trap

over the wooden bridge to join his brothers in the meadow.

All three of them ate yummy green grass, and they grew **bigger** and **fatter**, and happier every day!

The End

Rapunzel

Once upon a time, a man and his wife lived in a little cottage in the shadow of a tall tower. They were very poor, but very happy.

On the other side of their garden wall was a vegetable patch. It was full of tasty-looking carrots, cabbages, and tomatoes. But there was never anyone in the patch.

"Why should all those vegetables go to waste when we're hungry?" the man asked his wife.

79

So he climbed over the wall and quickly filled his basket. As he pulled a carrot out of the ground, he heard an angry voice.

"Who said you could take MY vegetables?"

It was the old witch who owned the tower! She threatened to cast an evil spell on the man and his wife.

"Please don't hurt us," begged the man. "My wife is going to have a baby!"

"I will let you go," said the witch, "but you must give me the baby when it is born. I will care for it and treat it as my own."

The man was so scared he agreed to everything the witch asked.

Soon, the man's wife had a baby girl, and the very next day, the witch took the baby away.

The witch named the baby **Rapunzel**.

83

The baby grew into a beautiful girl.

But when Rapunzel was twelve years old, the witch locked her in a room at the top of the tower, afraid that someone might take her away.

A year or two passed and Rapunzel grew taller and her hair grew longer.

Poor Rapunzel was lonely and wished she had a friend. She would gaze out of the window, looking at the beautiful forest outside, brushing her golden hair and singing sad, sweet songs to herself.

"How I wish the witch would set me free.
There's a great big world I long to see."

85

One day, a prince was riding in the forest near the tower. He heard Rapunzel singing and was enchanted by her voice.

The prince hid behind a bush and listened.

Soon, the witch arrived at the bottom of the tower and called out,

"Rapunzel, Rapunzel, let down your hair."

Beautiful Rapunzel appeared at the window and let down her long, golden hair for the witch to climb up.

The next day, the prince watched the witch slide down Rapunzel's hair. When he was sure that the witch was far away, the prince called out,

"Rapunzel, Rapunzel, let down your hair."

Down tumbled the long golden hair and up climbed the prince.

89

At first, Rapunzel was frightened of the stranger.
But they quickly became friends.

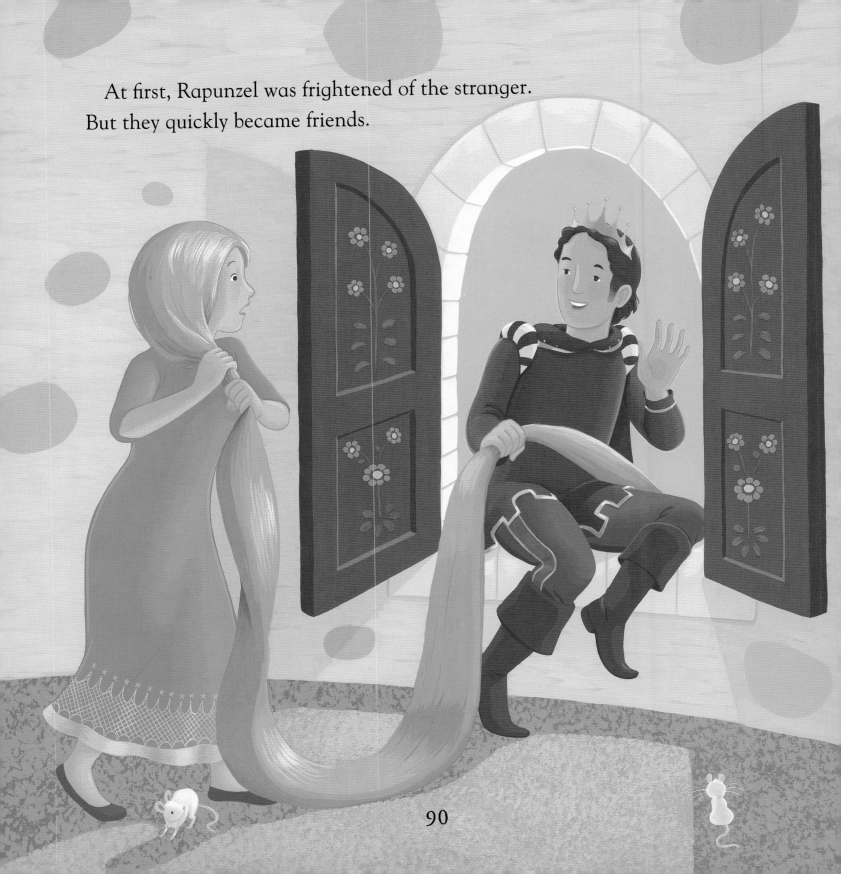

Rapunzel loved hearing the prince's stories.

He told her how it felt to run barefoot in a grassy meadow ...

and how it felt to swim in the cold, blue sea. Rapunzel had never done such things.

"I will help you escape from the tower," promised the prince.

The next day, and for many days after, the prince visited Rapunzel whenever the witch went out.

Every time, he would call out,

"Rapunzel, Rapunzel, let down your hair."

And every time, he brought silk string for Rapunzel to weave into a ladder so she could, one day, climb down the tower and escape.

Rapunzel worked on the ladder in secret and soon it nearly reached the ground.

The witch knew nothing of this until once, without thinking, Rapunzel said, "Oh, you are so much heavier than the prince when you climb!"

The witch was very angry.

94

She grabbed the scissors from Rapunzel's sewing basket and cut up the ladder.

SNIP! SNIP! SNIP!

Then the witch cut off Rapunzel's long, golden hair and cast a spell, banishing Rapunzel deep into the forest.

Still angry, the witch waited until she heard the prince call out,

"Rapunzel, Rapunzel, let down your hair."

Down to the ground tumbled Rapunzel's long, golden hair and up climbed the prince.

96

"Ha!" cried the witch, when the prince reached the top. "You've come for Rapunzel, but she has gone and you'll never find her!"

Shocked, the prince

f e l l

from the tower, into a thorn bush on the ground. The bush broke his fall but the thorns scratched his eyes, making him blind.

For many months, the blind prince wandered through the wilderness. Everywhere he went, he called, "Rapunzel! Rapunzel! Where are you?"

One day, he heard a sad, sweet song float through the woods.

"As I roam from tree to tree, My true love's face I long to see."

"Rapunzel! Rapunzel!" he called, "Is that you?"

Rapunzel ran through
the woods and hugged the prince.

"I've found you at last!" she cried.

Rapunzel's tears of joy fell into the prince's eyes
and he could see once more! Rapunzel's long hair was short now,
but she was still as beautiful as ever.

Rapunzel and the prince never saw the witch again and they traveled
the world together, visiting all the wonderful sights Rapunzel had longed
to see. And they lived **happily ever after!**

100

The End

Rumpelstiltskin

Once upon a time, there was a poor miller who had a beautiful daughter. Her eyes were the color of cornflowers and she had rosy pink cheeks. She was so lovely and clever that the miller couldn't resist telling everyone about her.

One day, the king rode through the village. The miller desperately wanted to impress the king.

"Your highness, my daughter is pretty and smart," he boasted.

But the king took no notice.

"She can also spin straw into gold!" the miller added, sure that this would get the king's attention.

103

"Whoa!"

The king stopped
his horse and
demanded to meet
the miller's daughter.

He took her back to his castle and led her up a winding staircase to a room in the turret. There, she found a spinning wheel and a towering pile of straw.

"Spin this straw into gold by morning," said the king, "or you'll be thrown into the dungeon!"

105

As soon as the king left, the miller's daughter began to cry. Even if she had a year to spin the straw into gold, she couldn't, for she didn't know how! Thinking about the dark, dingy dungeon, she sobbed even louder.

Just then, a funny little man danced into the room, clicking his heels and tapping his toes.

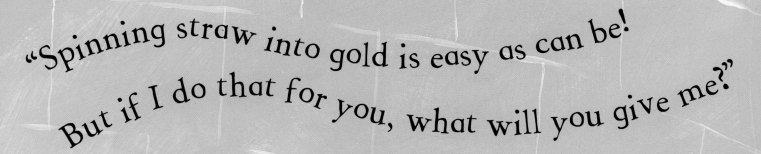

"Spinning straw into gold is easy as can be!
But if I do that for you, what will you give me?"

The miller's daughter offered the little man her necklace and, quick as a flash, he spun the straw into gold thread.

The next morning, the king was so pleased that he brought the girl an even bigger pile of straw! Again, he ordered her to spin it into gold by dawn.

Well, she still didn't know how to do it. Sure that she would be dragged to the dungeon, the miller's daughter wept.

And just as before, the funny little man jigged into the room.

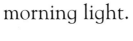

"Spinning straw into gold is easy as can be! But if I do that for you, what will you give me?"

This time, the miller's daughter gave the little man her ring. Quick as a flash, he spun the straw into gold thread that gleamed in the morning light.

109

The king was delighted,
and wanted more.

He brought
the girl a
pile of straw
so TALL
it reached
the ceiling!

She was to spin it into gold by sunrise.

Once more, the girl cried and the funny
little man hopped and skipped into the room.

"Spinning straw into gold is easy as can be!
But if I do that for you, what will you give me?"

This time, the miller's daughter had nothing left to offer him.
He made her promise to give him her firstborn child. Then,
fingers flying and toes tapping, he spun the straw into gold.

The king was so overjoyed with
the golden thread that he asked the
miller's daughter to marry him!

They held the wedding the very next day and the miller almost burst with pride when his daughter became queen.

The king and queen were very happy and the miller was poor no longer.

A year after the wedding, the queen had a bonny baby boy. She had forgotten all about the funny little man and the promise she had made.

One day, while the queen hummed a lullaby, the funny little man danced into the nursery and demanded the baby prince.

"Oh, please don't take my son," the queen begged.

114

The little man thought for a moment. Then he clapped his hands and sang,

"You can keep the prince if you play my game—
You've got **three** days to guess my name!"

The queen lay awake all night, making a list of all the names she could think of.

116

That evening, the little man twirled into the nursery again.

"Is your name Harry?

Or Larry?

Or Barry?"

asked the queen.

But all of her guesses were wrong. The little man cackled with glee and sang,

"You can keep the prince if you play my game—
You've got **two** more days to guess my name!"

The next day, the queen sent messengers all over the land to find out more names.

Then, that evening, the little man appeared again.

"Are you named Tim?

Or Jim?

Or Kim?"

asked the queen.

Once again, all her guesses were wrong. The little man hooted with delight and sang,

"You can keep the prince if you play my game—You've got **one** more day to guess my name!"

The next day, the queen's servant
was chopping logs in the woods
when he heard a strange sound.
He ducked behind a pinetree and
watched a funny little man leaping
around a fire, singing ...

120

"The queen will never win this game—
For **Rumpelstiltskin** is my name!"

The servant hurried home to tell the queen what he had seen.

That evening, when the little man danced into the nursery, the queen pretended to think. "Hmm," she said. "Is your name ...

Doodlebug?

Or Tiddlywinks?

Or Flibbertigibbet?"

122

The little man shrieked with laughter and shook his head.

"Do you give up?" he asked, reaching for the baby.

"I know ... it's RUMPELSTILTSKIN!" exclaimed the queen.

123

The little man's face turned as red as a beet and he howled,

"Oh what a shame, what a terrible shame!
The queen knows Rumpelstiltskin's my name!"

Throwing himself to the floor, he kicked his feet and pounded his fists so hard that the boards splintered and split. Rumpelstiltskin tumbled through the floor—and was never seen again!

The End

Jack and the Beanstalk

Once, there was a boy named Jack who lived with his mother. They were very poor and had to sell their cow to get money for food.

As he was taking the cow to market, Jack met an old man.

"You won't get much money for such an old cow," he told Jack, "but I can give you something better than money for her—magic beans!"

He held out his hand and showed Jack five speckled beans.

"Magic beans!" thought Jack. "They sound exciting!"

He gave the old man the cow and took the beans, thanking the man politely. Then he went home to his mother.

Jack's mother was extremely cross.

"Silly boy!" she shouted.

"Thanks to you,
we have no cow
and no money!"

She threw the beans out of the
window and sent Jack straight to bed.

129

The next morning, Jack was astonished when he looked out of the window. A giant beanstalk had sprung up while he was sleeping, and it stretched up to the sky.

Jack ran outside and began to climb the beanstalk.

Up and up he went, higher

and higher, till he reached the top.

There he found a road,
which led to a big house.

131

Jack's tummy was rumbling with hunger, so he knocked on the large, wooden door.

A giant woman answered. She looked kind and Jack asked if she would give him some breakfast.

"You will BE breakfast if my husband finds you!" she told Jack. "He's much bigger than me, and he eats children!"

But Jack begged and pleaded, and at last the woman let him in. She gave him some bread and milk and hid him in a cupboard.

Soon Jack heard loud footsteps and felt the cupboard shake. The giant man was coming! Jack heard him roar,

"Fee-fi-fo-fum, I smell the blood of an Englishman!"

"Don't be so silly," the giant's wife said. "You smell the sausages I've cooked for your breakfast! Now sit down and eat."

After wolfing down three plates of sausages, the giant asked his wife to bring him his gold. She brought two big sacks filled with gold coins, which the giant began to count. But he was sleepy after his big breakfast and soon began to snore.

Jack crept out of the cupboard and grabbed one of the sacks. Then he rushed out of the house, along the road, and straight down the beanstalk.

Jack's mother was overjoyed to see him, and she was even happier when she saw the gold.

They lived well while the money lasted, but after a year it had all been spent. Once again, Jack and his mother had nothing to eat.

"Don't worry, Mother," said Jack. "I'll just go back up the beanstalk to the giant's house."

And so he did. Just as before, Jack knocked on the door and begged the giant's wife for something to eat.

"Go away," she told him. "The last time you were here, a sack of gold disappeared. My husband was really cross!"

But once again, Jack begged and pleaded, and at last she let him in. She gave him some bread and milk and hid him in the cupboard.

Soon the giant stomped in, bellowing, "Fee-fi-fo-fum,

I smell the blood of an Englishman!"

"Nonsense," said the giant's wife.
"You smell the soup I've cooked
for your lunch."

Peeping through a crack in the cupboard door,
Jack saw the giant slurp down a big barrelful of soup,
and heard him tell his wife, **"Bring me my hen!"**

141

She put a fat red hen
on the table, and the
giant shouted,

"Lay!"

To Jack's
amazement,
the hen laid a
golden egg!

Jack waited until the giant was asleep.

"Zzzzzzzz!"

Then he jumped out and snatched the hen.
Fast as lightning, he dashed out of the house,

along the road...

and

down

the

beanstalk.

Jack and his mother lived very well on the money they made from the hen's golden eggs. But Jack wanted to climb the beanstalk one last time.

He knew the giant's wife would not let him in again, so when she wasn't looking, he sneaked into the house and crawled into the cupboard.

Before long, the giant came crashing in.

"Fee-fi-fo-fum, I smell the blood of an Englishman!"

he thundered.

"You smell the steaks I've cooked for your dinner," his wife said. And she put a platter of thick, juicy steaks in front of him.

After gobbling up the steaks, the giant took out a golden harp and said, **"Sing!"** The harp played a gentle lullaby, and soon the giant was fast asleep.

Jack sprang out, took the harp, and began to run. But the harp cried,

"Master! Master!"

... and the giant woke up.

With a roar, he leapt up and ran after Jack.

Holding the harp tightly, Jack ran for his life. As he scrambled down the beanstalk, he yelled,

"Mother! Mother! Bring the axe!"

Jack took the axe and started to chop down the beanstalk.

The giant quickly climbed back up to the top before it snapped in two.

That was the last time Jack saw him.

With the hen and the harp, Jack and his mother were able to live happily ever after—and they were never hungry again.

The End

The Little Mermaid

Once upon a time, deep beneath the sea, there lived a lovely Little Mermaid. She had long, chestnut hair, deep-sea-blue eyes and a beautiful fishtail of silvery green. She also had a voice as clear and bright as crystal, the most beautiful voice in the ocean.

The Little Mermaid lived with her father, the Sea King, and her five older sisters. She spent her days playing near their castle and singing to the other sea creatures.

On a mermaid's fifteenth birthday, she is allowed to go to the surface of the sea to watch the human world.

When it was the Little Mermaid's turn, she swam up eagerly.

A ship was sailing nearby. As the Little Mermaid
listened to the music and laughter, she saw a handsome
young prince. The Little Mermaid looked at him and
felt her heart melt with love.

The Little Mermaid followed the ship from a distance,
so that she could watch the young prince.

Suddenly, lightning FLASHED across the sky

and thunder CRACKED.

A fierce storm blew up, and the ship tossed and turned in the waves.

The Little Mermaid watched as it sank, hoping that the prince was safe.

When the storm was over, the Little Mermaid saw
her prince at last. He was lying in the water
with his eyes closed, too tired to swim.

"I must save him," the Little Mermaid thought.

She swam to him and took him to the safety of the shore. There she sang to him in her lovely, sweet voice until he opened his eyes.

He caught only a glimpse of her before she darted away to hide in the water.

Before long, a pretty girl came down to the beach. She found the prince and helped him up.

The Little Mermaid watched them walk away together. Then, with an aching heart, she swam back to her home.

With tears in her eyes, the Little Mermaid told her sisters that she had fallen in love with the prince. They knew who he was, and took her to see his home—a castle the color of sand, with steps winding down to the sea.

After that, the Little Mermaid swam to the
surface every day to watch the prince. "I would
do anything to be human so that he might fall in
love with me," she told her sisters.

161

Finally, her sisters said, "Go and visit the Sea Witch. Perhaps she can help you."

The Sea Witch lived in a dark underwater forest, amid slimy plants that looked like snakes. The Little Mermaid was frightened, but the thought of the prince made her brave.

"I can give you a potion that will make you human," said the Sea Witch. "But if you take it, you will lose your beautiful voice. You will get it back only if you win the true love of the prince."

163

The Little Mermaid took the potion
from the Sea Witch, and went home to say
goodbye to her father and sisters.

They were sad that she was leaving, but they all wished her happiness on land.

"Always remember where you come from," her father told her, "and come back to see us once a year." The Little Mermaid promised that she would.

Then she drank the witch's potion and swam to the surface, where she fell asleep on the soft sand below the prince's castle.

When the Little Mermaid awoke, her beautiful tail was gone, and in
its place were two long, slender legs. She was wearing a pretty gown, the
same silvery green as her tail, and on her feet were two silver slippers.

166

As she tried to stand up, the Little Mermaid's new legs wobbled, and she stumbled.

Suddenly, she was caught by two strong arms. She looked up—right into the eyes of the handsome prince.

168

"It's you!" the prince cried. "You are the girl who saved me from drowning, aren't you? I have been looking everywhere for you!"

The Little Mermaid nodded. But she could not say a word.

"Why won't you speak to me?" the prince asked, puzzled.

The Little Mermaid couldn't answer. She could only look at the prince and hope that he could see how much she loved him.

And he did. As he gazed into her deep-sea-blue eyes, the prince knew that she was the girl he had been looking for.

"I don't care if you can't speak," he told her. "I know that I love you more than anyone on earth. Will you marry me and live with me forever?"

The Little Mermaid's eyes shone, and she nodded. Then, as the prince kissed her, a wonderful thing happened. She could feel her voice returning!

"Yes," she said happily, "I will marry you!"

They were married the next day, and the Little Mermaid took the name Marina, which means "from the sea."

At their wedding, the prince took her in his arms and whirled her across the sand. Marina's new legs danced beautifully.

Every year on her birthday, Marina went down to the seashore and sang in her beautiful, crystal-clear voice.

Her father and sisters came up to see her, and were glad to know that Marina and her prince would live happily ever after.

The End

173

The Elves and the Shoemaker

Once upon a time, a shoemaker lived with his wife above his workshop.

The shoemaker was a good man, and he worked hard, but he was very poor. The day came when he had only enough leather to make one pair of shoes.

He cut out the leather and then left it on his workbench.

"I will be able to make a better pair of shoes after I've had a good night's sleep," he told his wife as they went upstairs.

175

The next morning, bright and early, the shoemaker went downstairs.

What a surprise he had!

On his workbench, where the leather had been, there was a **brand-new pair of shoes.** They were neatly and perfectly made, with not a stitch out of place.

"These shoes are masterpieces!" the shoemaker exclaimed to his wife.
He put them in the window, hoping someone would come and buy them.

Sure enough, a finely dressed young man soon entered the workshop to try on the shoes. They fitted perfectly, and they were so handsome that the man happily paid a high price for them.

With the money, the shoemaker was able to buy enough leather to make two new pairs of shoes.

By the time he returned to his shop, he was tired, so he cut out the leather and left it on his workbench. Then he went upstairs to bed.

179

The next morning, the shoemaker had another surprise!
There on the workbench were TWO new pairs of shoes!
They were even more beautiful than the first pair, and were just
as perfectly made.

The shoemaker put them in the window, and before lunchtime
he had sold both pairs for a very good price.

Now he had enough money to buy leather for four pairs
of shoes.

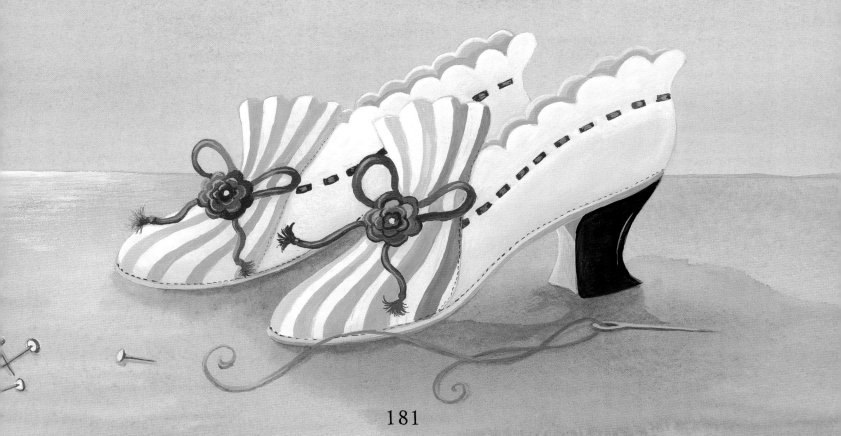

Once again, he cut out the leather, left it on his workbench, and went upstairs to bed.

And once again, he came down the next morning to find **beautiful shoes**, all made up and perfectly stitched.

182

The same thing happened every day for weeks. The shoes were appearing as if by magic. "Let's try and find out who's been making them tonight," his wife suggested.

So that night, the shoemaker left
some leather, all cut out and ready to
sew, on his workbench as usual.

Then, instead of going to bed, he and his
wife hid behind a curtain at the back of the shop.

There they waited ... and waited ...
and waited.

The shoemaker and his wife were just about to go to bed when, at the stroke of midnight, the shop door opened, and in danced two tiny elves! They skipped up to the workbench, and quickly began sewing the leather into fine new shoes. As they worked, they sang,

"We will sew and we will stitch,
To help the shoemaker grow rich!"

Soon the shoes were finished and the little elves
leapt off the workbench and danced out of the shop.

"Those kind elves have helped us," said the
shoemaker, astonished. "We must repay them."

"Did you see how thin their clothes were?" his wife
asked. "And their little feet were bare! Those poor
little men must be freezing."

"Let's make some warm clothes for the elves, to
show how grateful we are," said the shoemaker.

The next day, the shoemaker's wife
knitted two cozy woolen jackets ...

two tiny scarves ...

and two pairs of warm pants.

The shoemaker used his finest leather
to make two little pairs of boots.

That night, instead of leaving leather on his workbench, the shoemaker left the clothes, all wrapped up in shiny paper and ribbons. Then he and his wife hid behind the curtain to wait.

At the stroke of midnight, the shop door opened, and in came the little elves.

They hopped up onto the workbench, and saw the presents that had been left for them.

They opened the parcels at once, and in the twinkling of an eye, they had dressed in their brand-new clothes. They knew that the presents were the shoemaker's way of saying thank you, and they did a happy dance together, singing,

"Now the shoemaker's grown rich,
There's no need to sew and stitch."

Then they hopped off the workbench and scurried out the door.

The shoemaker and his wife never saw the little elves again. But their troubles were over, and they had a good and happy life together for many long years.

The End